4 Short Romance Stories Collection #4 Copy

Sweet and Clean & Wholesome, Easy to Read Fiction

Misha Quinn

Disclaimer

The characters and events portrayed in this book are fictitious. Any similarity to real persons, living or dead, is coincidental and not intended by the author. No part of this book may be reproduced, or stored in a retrieval system, or transmitted in any form or by any means, electronic, mechanical, photocopying, recording, or otherwise, without express written permission of the publisher.

Disclaimer for External Links

These links are being provided as a convenience and for informational purposes only; they do not constitute an endorsement or an approval by the Publisher or the Author of this book of any of the products, services or opinions of the corporation or organization or individual. The publisher bears no responsibility for the accuracy, legality or content of the external site or for that of subsequent links. Contact the external site for answers to questions regarding its content.

NO AI TRAINING

Publisher: Independently published

Cover design by: Canva Pro & Misha Quinn

COPYRIGHT

Blurbs - Romance Short Story Collections

Romance stories in these collections are short stories or even flash fiction.
It is feel-good fiction with warm feelings, hope, and twists in the love storyline.
These short stories are easy to read, with short paragraphs and large print paperback editions that suit the elderly and those who need to focus more when reading. LARGE PRINT edition paperbacks are also a nice present for seniors and people who need bigger fonts.

ROMANCE SHORT STORY COLLECTIONS SERIES - A Heartwarming, Feel-Good, Easy-Read Fiction Series – with LARGE PRINT paperback editions

https://books2read.com/5shortRomanceStoriesCollection1

https://books2read.com/shortromancestories2

https://books2read.com/shortromancestories3

https://books2read.com/shortromancestories4

https://books2read.com/shortromancestories5

https://books2read.com/shortromancestories6-1

Contents

Mary and the Pigeons

The sky was cloudless and blue. A flock of pigeons flew in circles in it. The girl stood in the house's courtyard, tilting her head, watching their flight.

Everything about this flock of pigeons was beautiful: some were tumbling, gradually descending, and soaring upward again. Others were rising higher and higher in a spiral and almost disappearing in the sunrise.

The girl, Mary, stood in the house's courtyard, tilting her head, watching their flight. You would think the whole life of these birds was about pleasing people.

Mary was a severe pigeon breeder, devoting all her free time to her pigeons. Having lost her father, whose pigeons were his joy, she did not sell the flock but continued to care for it and compete with her neighbors.

It seemed to the girl that her whole life depended on how high her flock of pigeons flew and on how many somersaults the best of her birds could do. One thing was sure: watching the flight of her birds or sitting in the pen at the pigeon house, Mary forgot all her troubles and her longing for her father. She thought he was beside her, watching their pigeons.

But there was another reason for all this: Mary underestimated herself and was not used to the attention of men. She dressed in baggy clothes and used no makeup at all. Her friends did not share her fascination with pigeons. They looked more at how they would be appreciated by potential life partners - guys from their neighborhood.

And Mary did not notice the boys at all. Of course, she had boys as her only friends at school. Still, when everyone grew up and started dating, Mary was utterly absorbed in caring for her pigeon house and fell out of the circle of boys' socializing.

Many people practiced pigeons in a town on the banks of a mountain river. For the people of her neighborhood, located right on the side of a large hill by the river, pigeons were a hobby that gave a sense of freedom and flight. Even Mary's house, on a narrow stone-paved street at the top of this hill, was a very favorable place for pigeon keeping. It was easier for a flock of pigeons to rise above the other flocks because, compared to the neighboring flocks, they had to fly fifty meters less to reach a good height at which it was possible to show dives and somersaults.

But one secret the girl was hiding tormented her. Mary did not know how to lure pigeons from other people's flocks. And that kept her in suspense.

What was the matter if everyone could buy a good enough pigeon in the market?

The reason for this was sporting interest: whoever could lure another pigeon and keep it in his flock for a long time, or perhaps forever, was the coolest pigeon keeper. Of course, it was not stealing; it was believed that in this way, they gave the tired pigeon a chance to join the new flock and, together with it, to fly into the pigeon cote and get food and rest. After all, if a pigeon was separated from its flock, it needed to be more experienced or energized. Perhaps the bird was carried by intense winds far from where it usually flew and did not have the energy to return immediately. In their foothill region, strong wind squalls were not uncommon. The gorge from which the mountain river flowed worked like a tunnel, and the wind could crush it.

So that the new pigeon would not fly away anywhere again, it was kept only in the pigeon cote for some time so that it would find a mate and get used to the new place.

If the owner came looking for his pigeon, of course, the bird would be given back. But if the owner was not so attentive to his flock and did not notice that his pigeon was missing, the bird was left with the new owner. Everything was fair from the point of view of the pigeon breeding community.

And now Mary noticed in the sky, close to her flock of pigeons. This lone pigeon was approaching in a large arc uncertainly to the other pigeons circling above her pigeon cote.

The girl froze: here it was, her first opportunity to lure a pigeon! Her heart raced as if she were expecting some pleasant surprise. Her palms were a little sweaty, and she wiped them hastily on her pants. The girl looked around and saw a bucket of whole grains, which she was sprinkling on the floor of the pigeon cote so that the pigeons would return to their place as soon as possible. Mary rushed to the bucket and scooped up a handful of grains with her hand. Then she looked up into the sky again, looking for that strange pigeon. It was there and flying near her flock, still hesitant to join their circle. But Mary realized bringing the alien down to earth with her flock would be possible.

Incredibly, from a height of many dozens of meters, the pigeons could see tiny grains falling on the platform of their pigeon cote.

Mary had always been fascinated by the birds' keen eyesight, and she used it to get the pigeons to return to the pigeon cote. Why was this important? Because if a thunderstorm or severe weather with fierce winds was coming, it would be difficult for the pigeons to get back. Some of them could be carried quite far by the wind. Not all of them, but the ones that were weaker or younger.

Therefore, to bring the flock down to the ground faster, the pigeon chicks were taught from their "teenage years" that when grain was thrown on the ground, it meant that it was time for the adult pigeons to return and thus to be the first to eat the unique grain, which they did not get at other feeding times.

And so, Mary threw grains on the floor of the pigeon cote and watched as the first pigeons from her flock, which flew lower than the others, had already spiraled back down to her pigeon cote.

When the new pigeon landed on the floor of the dovecote, Mary sat back and did not move. She did not want to scare the bird away.

The guest was beautiful - a proud head with huge nostrils, a beautiful color - white with red - and strong legs. There was no ring on him - the owner had not marked his bird. Mary watched as the pigeon greedily pounced on the food. Perhaps it had been away from its home for a long time, hungry, was it?

Mary stood up and cautiously approached the pigeons, who had already had their grain filled, and corralled them inside the pigeon cote to rest. The new pigeon only dared to enter the pigeon box for a short time. But he followed them all and hid in it. Mary knew he would find a place there, for the pigeon cote had enough room for ten new pigeons and their nests.

"It worked!"

Mary jumped up and down on one foot when she closed the pigeon cote door. What she was going to do with the new pigeon, she did not know.

"It's just that he'll stay with me for a while, and maybe he'll find a mate among the young lovebirds that have just matured," she thought as she walked back to the yard of her house.

Her house, on the slope of a hill, was built as an extended structure, surrounded by a street whose sidewalk rose to its side windows and on the other by a garden. Mary sat in her room and did not look at what her mother and cousins did in the yard. She was pleased, and this elated mood lasted for a long time.

After a few days, the girl noticed the new pigeon was already courting the cote. This meant he was doing well, and soon, he could be released with his new mate to fly with the whole flock. No one had come for the dove yet, and this anticipation of a possible unpleasant moment gradually dissolved into the daily chores that filled Mary's life. But then, one day, Mary went out to open the door for the mailman, and the first question he asked was, "I hear you have a new tenant?"

Mary did not get the humor and replied. "There's no one new here. Can't you see that the same old tenants are still here?"

But the letter carrier, an elderly man bringing them mail for many years, immediately explained.

"And I'm not talking about you. I'm talking about the pigeon you took in."

Mary's insides felt as if they had collapsed. Her heart plunged downward and froze. Yes, she released an alien pigeon into the sky yesterday, and it returned. All was well, but, someone in the neighborhood had noticed a new color of pigeon flying in her flock, one she had not had before.

"Oh, those neighbors are pigeon fanciers!" thought the girl.

Embarrassed, she mumbled back.

"Yeah, there's a guy hanging around... so what?"

The mailman continued, staring at her. "That's probably the best pigeon in my nephew's flock, Nico."

Now, Mary was ready to fall to the ground in shame.

"But I didn't want to keep him by force. He's already found a mate..." was all she could mutter before the letter carrier hastily stopped her. "Come on, I didn't mean to offend you! On the contrary, thank you for saving the pigeon from starvation. We live so far away from your area that a pigeon wouldn't have been able to come back on his own for a long time. Then, he would probably have starved to death in the wilderness around our town or been caught by a falcon or other bird of prey."

He sighed heavily and continued.

"And besides, we can't do the flock anymore. We'll probably give it to other pigeon breeders."

Mary looked up at the letter carrier, startled by his words.

"Do you mean you'll give up your pack? What happened?"

The mailman lowered his head and replied quietly, "Nico ended up in the hospital for a long time. He can't do pigeons anymore, and me and his parents don't have the time or energy for it. We're old now."

Mary anxiously continued her questioning.

"What happened to your nephew, Nico?"

The mailman replied. “He… got into a fight with local thieves, and they broke his arm in two places, despite his knowledge of fighting techniques. He was defending a woman who was attacked by bandits and had her bag snatched from her rack. He caught up with one of them and forced him to drop the bag, but the others came at him and…”

Mary felt a keen sense of guilt toward this man whose relative had suffered so much for justice, and she had baited their pigeon. She did not feel now that she had saved the bird. It seemed she had stolen it and deserved, if not punishment, repentance.

“I must give you your pigeon right away,” said the girl, preparing to turn and return to the pigeon cote to bring the pigeon to the letter carrier immediately.

“No, no, I’m not taking the pigeon away. I didn’t mean to. I need to say something to Nico about what’s wrong with his pet. He’s so worried… Unfortunately, the guy’s arm isn’t recovering well - the fractures are severe, and he won’t be able to go home for a long time.”

Mary suddenly felt an extraordinary rush of feelings - sympathy, tenderness, and duty to Nico, a stranger to her who had been so brave as to protect the woman without sparing himself. The girl said,

"Can I visit your Nico? I'll tell him what happened to his pigeon."

The mailman looked at her in surprise.

"You? But why not? Of course, you can tell him about the pigeon yourself. I think he'll be glad to hear it firsthand. Besides, I won't be able to visit him until a few days later. I've got a long shift this week, and I don't have the energy to go to him in the evenings. I'll give you the address of the hospital where he is and the room number. You can come to see him in the afternoon, from about four o'clock until seven in the evening."

He dug into the pocket of his bag and handed Mary a crumpled piece of paper with the hospital's address on it. The girl took the note from the letter carrier's hands and, bidding him a warm farewell, closed the wicket door of the yard. Then she went to the pigeon house and sat there for a long time, listening to the cooing of the pigeons and looking at the white and red pigeons with a pang of disappointment.

The next day, Mary arrived at the hospital. She was allowed into Niko's room and did not have to explain anything except that she had important business.

The girl timidly entered the room. The young man was lying in bed. His right arm was in plaster and suspended on some bracket above the bed. A look of longing on his strong-willed face, with its prominent cheekbones and stubborn mouth, did not fit with what Mary had heard about his bravery.

But as she looked around the room, she realized there was much to pine for. Instead of his pigeons, Niko saw only a piece of sky from the ward window. The tall buildings of the downtown district obscured everything else.

Mary stepped timidly into the room and, approaching Nico's bed, said,

"Hello, Nico. I'm Mary."

The guy, who at first paid no attention to the visitor, turned away from the window and looked at her in surprise as he answered the greeting.

"Hello, Mary. But we've never met, so how do you know my name?"

The girl was embarrassed, but now there was nowhere to go, so she blurted out,

"I have your pigeon. Your uncle said you'd like to know that..."

Nico tried to pull himself up on the bed but could not and leaned back on the pillow again. "Wow, what a surprise!" He replied, smiling. "I didn't realize we had girls doing pigeons, too."

There was both surprise and mockery in his voice. This took Mary aback, and she answered proudly.

"Yes, I have pigeons. They were left to me after my father..."

Nico realized he had offended his guest and hurriedly apologized.

"I'm sorry, I didn't know. Of course, my wounded pride as an avid pigeon fancier made me say that."

He showed her to the chair beside the bed with his healthy hand.

Mary timidly sat down on its edge. She had to find the strength to get on with the business she had come for.

"I wish I could give you your pigeon back. But he's... it's been a couple of weeks, and he's got..."

"A pigeon showed up?" Nico smiled, looking at the even more embarrassed girl.

He liked her more - her directness, openness, and inability to call things by their proper names.

"Yes, your pigeon..." she muttered.

Nico pressed his lips together in feigned thoughtfulness and said, regarding Mary,

"Well, since that's the case, let him stay. My uncle told me that my Caesar - the name of this pigeon - was lost after the family started the flock flying just before a thunderstorm.

Caesar, who, as always, flew higher than everyone else, was carried away by the wind and couldn't come back - not that day or later. When did he fly to you?"

"Two weeks ago, Tuesday," Mary exhaled, looking at Nico with relief and interest.

"Yeah, he's been without food for a few days. Thanks for saving his life."

Nico's voice sounded of sincere gratitude. He looked at Mary with appreciation.

The girl blushed with embarrassment and with pleasure. Niko, who had saved another human at the cost of his health, thanked her for saving his pigeon! Mary felt a pleasant feeling fill her heart - a sense of understanding and gratitude to Niko for not even thinking of accusing her of stealing the pigeon.

The girl muttered.

"I thought that... I just wanted to bring a new pigeon into the pigeon cote for the first time - straight from the sky. You know, it's almost like a sport, a competition between pigeon keepers..."

Nico realized the girl was utterly embarrassed and hastily replied.

"I know and understand everything. We've had pigeons for years, and I've done that too - baited other pigeons. Some came home. Some stayed forever. And you know, Caesar is the son of one such alien. So he repeated the fate of his father, who still lives in my flock and flies well. So, I don't condemn anyone for doing such things. I thank you sincerely, Mary, for saving this pigeon."

Mary felt a blush flood her cheeks, not of shame, as she had at first, but of pleasure. She no longer had to be ashamed of the motives behind her actions with Caesar. This noble young man had lifted from her soul the great weight of guilt that had crushed her yesterday when his uncle had said Caesar was their dove.

Nico was the first to break the lingering silence.

"Shall we let Caesar live life to the fullest?" Mary laughed with relief, appreciating the joke.

Niko could only stare out the window, but his pet pigeon could live, fly, and love again.

The girl replied.

“Sure. Do you want me to tell you how Caesar appeared in the sky above my dovecote?”

Nico nodded silently, smiling, and made himself comfortable in bed, ready to listen to a long story. He hoped it would be extended because he wanted Mary to stay with him longer.

The girl moved closer to his bed and began her story, excitedly describing everything that had happened on the day Caesar had appeared in the sky next to her flock of doves.

The nurses who passed by the open door of Niko’s hospital room eyed the strange visitor, dressed in almost boyish clothes, with interest. Their patient had never shown much interest in any young woman, delighted with the act that had brought him here. But here he was, sitting in front of some angular girl who looked like a sparrow and smiling at her as if... As if Niko saw his fate and happiness in her.

THE END

Written by Misha Quinn, 2023

Cecilia and the Sea God

The sea was splashing with complete indifference to the one who had devoted herself to serving it. Well, not the sea, but sailing. And what did she, Cecilia, have left now? Nothing...

A full but well-shaped middle-aged woman sat with her mermaid tail hanging down from the jetty's edge and looked out at the surf. The waves were lapping at the beach in the early morning, before sunrise, yet filled with tourists vacationing in the resort.

And what would change in her life if many people were on that beach? Nothing. All these people were strangers to her. They were just clients for whom Cecilia gave her performances, one after the other, with short breaks for the opportunity to take off her elaborate mermaid outfit and take a break.

Cecilia knew she should not work so hard but could not help it. Swimming, especially as a mermaid, had been her passion since childhood. Cecilia thought about the fact that she had been dragged to the pool by her friends, who were always telling her she should lose weight and, to do so, she should exercise vigorously.

Cecilia followed their advice, became a professional athlete, and won many competitions in different styles of swimming. But most of all, she liked swimming underwater - calmly, sliding her body, without the high loads and training usual for competitive swimmers.

Yes, about her weight... Cecilia's weight was never close to ideal. But the girl was not discouraged, and everything in her life went according to plan - first love, marriage... but she and her husband had no children, and something in the relationship broke down. The couple separated. Cecilia and her first husband separated without scandals and disputes about the division of property, which was already an achievement.

Cecilia, who had completed her college education by the time she divorced her first husband, went to work as a nurse in a hospital. She found time to swim in the pool in her spare time between shifts. One day, while watching a television program about the entertainment world, she saw an interview with a professional mermaid.

"Wow, is there such a thing?" thought the young woman, and after finding a company that made mermaid clothing for the customer's measurements, she ordered and received her first mermaid costume. Everything about the outfit was perfect. After immediately trying out her mermaid costume in the pool, Cecilia decided that from now on, she would work part-time as a mermaid at parties.

This part-time job, which she did in her spare time, brought her more pleasure than money. However, in the world of enthusiastic people, Cecilia found like-minded people and friends who did not pay any attention to her unusual weight for a mermaid. They valued Cecilia's balanced character and love for their shared passion - the world of mermaids. Gradually, Cecilia switched to working as a mermaid and constantly looked for opportunities to get work orders. There were few, but the party for the children, which was organized yesterday in the hotel complex of this sea resort, was well paid and greatly pleased the children and her.

"So what's the matter? Why am I depressed?" Cecilia thought, looking at the waves. "Am I so lacking in simple human warmth and tenderness? Have I not learned to live without a man in my life? Or is it just my body that wants affection and tenderness so much?"

Cecilia sighed heavily and, leaning one hand on the pier's edge, deftly jumped into the sea.

The seawater gripped her body tightly and rocked her in its waves.

The woman was lying face up in the water, arms wide open, looking up into the morning sky. Not all the stars had yet been extinguished in the pale morning sky. The saltwater was so dense compared to the freshwater of the pool that Cecilia was pleased to feel that she did not have to make any effort to stay on the water's surface despite her mermaid garb. Usually, Cecilia would take care of her costume and not swim in the salty sea water that was gradually eating away the paint from the surface of her outfit.

The woman turned face down, opened her eyes in the water, and, trying not to make any sudden movements, tried to see what was happening around her. And underwater, there was a lot to see. An arc of pink light was rising from the bottom of the sea. Then, it was a dome glowing with pink light. A human-like figure was visible in its center.

"Someone must be scuba diving here. But why so early?" thought Cecilia, relieved it was not a shark. "The air from his breathing apparatus must have created this dome effect around the diver rising from the sea depths."

"Actually, why not? After all, I've been swimming in the sea since early morning, too, and in my work clothes," Cecilia continued to ponder, returning to her relaxed state.

The woman spread her arms out again and closed her eyes as she floated on the water's surface. Suddenly, something touched Cecilia - as if someone's hand lightly ran a palm across her back.

"And what are you doing here?" A low male voice suddenly sounded right in her ear. "I wasn't expecting anyone to visit this morning."

The stranger's voice sounded a little mocking and surprised.

Cecilia turned upright in the water in surprise, but her mermaid tail resisted the water, and it failed. The woman twisted around in the water, trying to get into a position where she could see the unexpected guest better.

And the man, perfectly upright in the water, floated beside her and looked mockingly at the woman.

Cecilia finally found a position to stay upright in the water and swam up to the man, helping herself with her arms.

At first, Cecilia thought it was a scuba diver. But as soon as she saw him... Wow, the man was not wearing scuba equipment but even ordinary swimming trunks. In the relatively clear water of the sea bay, Cecilia could see his mighty torso and whole body below. And that body was... wow, she found her colleague - this man with a fishtail instead of legs.

The woman smiled at the stranger and immediately felt that there was something between them that connected them. They shared a common hobby - swimming as mermaids - and that was so rare! Cecilia had only one male acquaintance among professional mermaids, and he was lovely. But he was not her type, so Cecilia did not expect their relationship to go beyond mere acquaintance.

And here... oh God, she loved everything about him: a broad smile, his long dark curly hair that fell in heavy waves over the mighty shoulders of a great swimmer.

She could not take her eyes off him, so singularly blue beneath the black lashes. His eyebrows were perfection itself, thick, spreading apart like the wings of an albatross. His nose was straight, with a slight hump that gave away the proud character of a lord of the seas.

Cecilia thought he would have played Poseidon better than in the movie she'd seen recently. Yes, that actor had been good, but this man was just the epitome of a sea god. Or was it the surprise of meeting such a handsome man that made Cecilia think that?

The woman looked embarrassed and finally responded to her guest's greeting.

"Well, I wasn't expecting you... I'm resting here. Haven't you noticed that?"

There was a playful note in the woman's voice. Cecilia felt the sudden change in her voice, how it became chestier and longer.

The stranger floated beside her and stared at her unwaveringly. He gawked. Her face, then his gaze, traveled lower... under the water. He could see her mermaid costume, but the stranger did not seem surprised. He said,

"I see I have interrupted your enjoyment of this beautiful morning. I'm sorry!"

He turned to swim away from Cecilia, but she immediately called out to him.

"No, don't go! No..."

There was so much pleading in her voice that the man turned to her and swam closer again. His gaze was so tender and understanding that Cecilia dared to say what was in her heart.

"I don't want to be alone... this morning. My name is Cecilia, and yours?" she said.

"Nice to meet you. My name is Poseidon."

Somehow, Cecilia was not surprised by the name. "Good alias," she said, looking understandingly at the man in his dark eyes.

"That suits you. Well, in that case, I'm a Mermaid," she said.

There was sarcasm and some disappointment in the woman's voice.

"Why is he lying? Doesn't he want to be called by his real name? It means he doesn't like me..." she thought, unable to tear her gaze away from the stranger hypnotizing her.

But the man immediately answered, and his voice was amiable, just as it had been at the beginning of their conversation.

"Why should it be a pseudonym? It's my name," the man replied and grinned.

Cecilia was embarrassed. She did not know what to say to correct her mistake. She struggled to get the words out without looking the man in the eye.

"I'm sorry, I didn't mean to offend you..." The man continued. "Believe me, my name is Poseidon. And I know your name is Cecilia. You don't have to be afraid of me. I'm not a demon, just a Sea God."

Cecilia stared dumbfounded at her new acquaintance. Okay, the man could have any name, but how did he know everything about her? At first, she thought the new acquaintance was continuing to taunt her. And he was doing it because she was so unattractive. After all, real mermaids are all slender, and she was the only one, a woman "in a body," who was often mocked by her acquaintances because of that. Why was it that only she thought this Poseidon was better than other men who usually just wanted to have fun with her without the long-term relationship she had sought after her first failed marriage? And this type is the same, just mocking her.

The man seemed to understand the doubts that tormented her and, holding his hand to Cecilia, said conciliatingly, “I am not mocking you. I am the Sea God, Poseidon. Look!”

He waved his hand, and something huge, glowing with lights, rose from the depths of the sea. The woman looked down into the water. An ancient sailing ship approached them, and all its sails were in place.

“How is that possible?” Cecilia thought. “It’s a ghost ship...”

Cecilia still could not believe her eyes.

“Am I dreaming?” She thought, but an extraordinary sense of wonder simultaneously filled her soul.

“No, I’m seeing all of this for real. But even if it is a dream, I wish it wouldn’t end...” the woman thought.

Poseidon held his hand to her, and she took it without hesitation. The man pulled Cecilia down into the water toward the ship. Cecilia did not think about how long she could stay underwater. The human ability to swim without breathing apparatus is minimal - it is only minutes. But she was so eager to be on this marvelous ship that she dived into the seawater, following her new acquaintance.

"Wow, his name is Poseidon, though," she thought, pointing down towards the ship. "But now he can be a god, and I can be his companion. Let it be only for a moment, but I shall feel happy beside him."

The woman dived in with Poseidon. In a couple of seconds, they were on the deck of the sailing ship, whose hulk rose ever higher and soon showed above the water's surface. The water ran off the deck, on which Poseidon led the way to the captain's cabin, which towered above the rest of the ship and seated Cecilia in one chair that stood there. He lay down on the boardwalk at her feet.

The man leaned back on the floor and, looking at Cecilia with a satisfied look, settled his fishtail and swung his arm again.

The most extraordinary sea creatures Cecilia had ever imagined appeared on the deck. There were handsome men with flippers on their feet, not flippers, but webbing! And the webs were not only on their feet but also on their arms.

Then the mermaids appeared on deck, carried by giant octopuses on nets suspended like hammocks between their tentacles. Each mermaid had her peculiar coloring - if she had red hair, her body was copper. If she had blue hair, her body would be blue. Her body was shimmering with all shades of red as if she had pink hair. But the main thing about their image was that they held themselves completely naturally and were not at all embarrassed to meet an earthly woman in the company of their lord.

Each of the mermaids sent an air kiss to Cecilia, and the octopuses arranged their charges so that each could talk to Poseidon and his companion if she wished.

Cecilia did not know where to look. Everything and everyone here was just like a fairy tale. The woman felt like she had entered one of the children's parks. But no human imagination could have created what was in front of her.

As more sea creatures came on deck, many borne by more brutal sea creatures like giant ocean crabs, Poseidon looked at Cecilia with a sidelong glance. He was studying his guest's reaction to what he had presented to her.

The woman silently accepted the greetings of his entourage. She nodded, responding to the bows or air kisses sent her way. Cecilia noticed that no earthly man who had ever stood before her could compare to Poseidon. His body was so perfect that it almost hurt her to look at him.

"But why would I look at a man who all the women of his kingdom desire? Even if he is a true Sea God, then what? I, who adore swimming and the sea, should worship him, but I feel something else besides mere admiration... I desire him, and it is utterly in vain. He'll never pay attention to me - I couldn't get a normal man to be my life partner, let alone a God," thought Cecilia.

A shadow of sadness appeared on her face. The woman lowered her head and stared at the floor haltingly.

Poseidon noticed the change in her mood. He dabbed his hand on her knee, the latex-covered artificial mermaid's tail, and said,

"I see you're sad. Don't you like my world?"

Cecilia, who shuddered at his touch, was embarrassed and replied, sliding her eyes over his face.

"No, no, I'm absolutely thrilled! I just..."

"Do you want to go home?" He continued questioning.

"No, no, not now. I can't..."

"To be compared to the beauty of my approaching ladies?" Poseidon asked slyly, looking affectionately at Cecilia.

"How does he know what I'm thinking? How?" She was confused, not knowing what to say to such a direct question. But yes - that was precisely what she had been thinking just a moment ago.

The Sea God continued.

"Pay no attention to them. They are the spawn of Water and Darkness, and you are the spawn of Earth and Light. You are completely different but so close. And that's because you're so fascinated with the sea. Have you ever wondered why you like the image of a mermaid so much?"

Cecilia stared at Poseidon in amazement, stunned by his words.

"No, I just like to swim..." she replied, looking at him expectantly.

The woman realized that her new acquaintance wanted to tell her something she did not know about herself.

Poseidon continued.

"There are mermaids in our midst who are born of mermaids. But some are born of men and come to us of their own accord."

"Oh, those aren't the ones that... drowned, are they?" Cecilia asked with a shudder.

Poseidon raised his eyebrows in surprise, then laughed in relief and replied.

"No, not those. Those mermaids who come to us of their own volition are like you. They are the ones who want to live exactly as we live underwater. But our lives are not just about celebrations and pleasures. We have enemies - those who claim the throne of ruler of the seas and those who would like to take all power on this planet into their own hands. So those who come to live in our world forever are fully aware of what they are walking into."

He was looking at Cecilia with a challenging gaze, clearly reading the thoughts on her face.

The woman sighed and felt frustrated as she thought that even if the possibility of coming to the Sea God's world war were real, at least in this dream she was in, she would have to leave her family behind. And she could not do that, as she loved them so much!

Cecilia realized she would not get such an offer from Poseidon again. And she raised her head firmly, looked straight into his eyes, and answered.

"I'd like that, but..."

"No need to go on, I understand," Poseidon interrupted her quietly. "What I have offered you is not the only solution. I can see that you are too attached to your earthly life - you have many relatives. But there's no way you'll find happiness on the shore..."

Cecilia was suddenly compelled to answer him with what she had just thought. There was a passion in the woman's voice that she had long held back and a sudden sense of hope for something vaguely formed in her mind.

"Yeah, I can't come to your world. What if you..."

Poseidon looked at her in surprise. Suddenly, he leaned toward her and whispered in her ear as if he were sharing a dream he had been hiding for a long time with Cecilia.

"You're right. I never thought of it the other way around. But with you, it seems possible..."

Cecilia stared at the sea god and barely listened to what he told her next. She needed to see him, to smell his scent, which the light sea breeze carried to her. Poseidon smelled of seawater, fresh morning breeze, and something unusual, spicy but light.

“Now I’ll wake up, and none of this will happen,” was the thought that kept running through Cecilia’s mind. “This is all my dream, my dreams. I wanted to be a mermaid so badly that I changed my whole life because of that passion. I haven’t had relationships with men in a long time, as none appeals to me anymore... not like this handsome man.”

“No one compares to him, no one,” she thought, wistful at this moment’s fleetingness.

Cecilia listened to Poseidon. She was already feeling the inevitability of the approaching parting with her whole body. Cecilia did not know what would happen next. They could not stay here, on this sailboat, unnoticed by anyone. Soon, there would be people on shore, and all she saw would disappear into the depths of the sea. And her new acquaintance, whether he called himself Poseidon or the Sea God, would also disappear from her life.

Meanwhile, Poseidon waved his hand again, and everything around him was misted. Cecilia felt like she was standing on the deck with both feet as if she was not wearing her mermaid clothes.

She looked down and realized she could see her feet. Instead of a mermaid's tail, she was wearing a swimsuit of an extraordinary blue color, covered with patterns embroidered with precious pearls.

Poseidon stood beside her. The woman realized they were no longer standing on the sailboat's deck but on the beach's sand from which she had swum out to sea. Cecilia suddenly realized he was as firmly on the ground as she was and no longer had a mermaid's tail. Her new acquaintance's muscular legs were spread wide, his arms at his sides like an experienced sailor.

Poseidon was wearing a swimmer's outfit - swim trunks and nothing else. He looked like an ordinary man now.

The woman looked at Poseidon in shock, her gaze reading an unspoken question that she did not even need to say out loud,

"Why? What's going to happen now? Have you... stayed with me here on earth?"

Poseidon silently held out his hand to her. Cecilia also silently extended her hand to him. Their hands joined.

Poseidon's hand was warm, his broad palm completely covering her small palm. Cecilia felt her heart beating somewhere in her throat from the excitement and strangeness of this moment. She did not know how much time Poseidon would spend with her as a man. Still, she was ready to accept at least a couple minutes of that happiness - to be near him, to feel his warmth and tenderness. That he would be gentle with her was clear from his treatment at the beginning of their meeting at sea.

Poseidon pulled Cecilia quickly behind him, away from the seashore. The woman and the man walked together along the yellow coastal sand towards the sunrise, the first rays of which had already brightened the cottages on the seashore and climbed higher and higher on their walls, penetrating everything around with the joy of the beginning of a new day.

This is how the love story of Poseidon and an ordinary earthly woman named Cecilia began. She no longer had to think about pleasing someone on purpose. Her man loved her with a special love, unconditionally, as she loved him.

THE END

Written by Misha Quinn, 2023

Aphrodite and Love

The beautiful Goddess of Love, Aphrodite, looked at the guy stomping at her feet. But in fact, the Goddess was not on Olympus but standing in a museum. And she was there in an image created for her by a talented sculptor of antiquity. This image was like a statue of a female figure made of white marble.

Although the body was marble in this incarnation, Aphrodite's soul was filled with feelings and memories. It was sculpted out of marble by a great sculptor thousands of years ago. Then, the statue was lost and found many millennia later. During this time, the skillful coloring and decorations of the figure had dissolved in the sands of time, and only white marble remained. But even this appearance was enough for people to appreciate again the beauty and greatness of the sculptor's idea.

Although the marble was cold and seemingly emotionless, this cold marble body was now quite fitting for Aphrodite. The Goddess of Love was everywhere and anywhere. Still, she often enjoyed moving into works of art and directly receiving the admirers' rapture of her beauty.

In principle, Aphrodite did not care how she was portrayed as long as the image evoked admiration and adoration of her eternal beauty. Many generations of women and men have appreciated and recognized the matchless beauty of Aphrodite - this is how the persona that the sculptor embodied in marble has been defined by historians and connoisseurs of art. Many took her image as the standard of female beauty.

However, Aphrodite recognized only the diversity of female forms, considering them the most exciting phenomenon of nature. Every day, hundreds of visitors pass by the statue of Aphrodite. Some of them passed by, glancing at her beautiful but almost naked body, and, embarrassed, hurried away. Others stopped before the statue and studied every inch for a long time, trying to find the answer to the question of true beauty.

Yes, Aphrodite's beauty was worshipped by more than one generation of women and men. Still, this worship was Aphrodite's habitual worship.

Today, however, Aphrodite was amused. She was amused by how a modern young man studied her statue. He was walking around, measuring the proportions of the figure of the Goddess' image and transferring it into a laptop. But there was no adoration or rapture in the gaze of this admirer. The young man was looking at the statue of the Goddess of Love rather indifferently. He measured it with some complicated-looking instruments and carefully entered the data of changes into the laptop.

Aphrodite was aware of the modern technology people use nowadays. She was well-versed in art and knew there was always good and bad style. It was not the first time she had been used to people walking around her in togas, then in tall hats and canes, and now in some strange clothes, the names she had not yet remembered.

However, people in the museum have yet to talk about these clothes.

Only women and men wore blue pants with pockets and seams, tuned with double stitching. These pants were tight or left their wearer's legs free depending on the current fashion. These clothes were like the workmen's clothes used a couple of centuries ago, first by sailors and then by common laborers.

Now, it seemed worn by everyone, men and women alike. Only a small select group of people who occasionally visited the museum dressed exquisitely and looked like aristocrats of the past. Now, in her opinion, this young man was one of those who dressed badly. He was wearing these awful blue pants with pants that were too wide.

Aphrodite looked at the strange museum visitor and thought about why he needed to measure the proportions of her sculpture. After all, in her opinion, no measurements would help to understand when the creator of an outstanding work of art would create a masterpiece and when he would create a hack, a so-called “common object.” Such an object does not need to be hackwork. It is simply what the creators say about what is made for sale based on the needs of the existing buyers and their tastes.

But what the painter or sculptor himself recognizes as a work of art - an object unique, which cannot be repeated, is often not sold or, in the lifetime of its creator, cannot get a proper appreciation from contemporaries.

It was such a unique work of art that this sculpture of Aphrodite, in which the soul of the Goddess of Love now lived, was impressive. During the lifetime of its creator, the sculpture was recognized as just an ordinary statue - another representation of the Goddess of Love. But as the millennia passed, most of the other statues of Aphrodite were lost, and those that survived to this day became rare and were recognized and worshipped worldwide by true admirers of art.

However, Aphrodite heard this strange guy turn to a girl in her early twenties who had just approached him.

"So, did you write it all down, Paola?"

The girl, without looking at the boy, replied.

"Yes, Raul, I wrote it all down. You're going to think I'm as clueless as..."

She did not finish. Paola's voice was full of ill-concealed irritation.

"She doesn't like the guy," Aphrodite thought with surprise.

However, this girl was interested in the Goddess. This young lady was short, dressed in dark-colored clothes, and looked like a modern goth. Still, not her appearance attracted attention, but her intelligent gaze could be seen if you looked closely at her face.

In addition, the lack of piercings and tattoos suggested that this museum visitor needed help understanding the image she was attracted to. That the girl had no tattoos was already said a lot. Aphrodite knew tattoos meant a lot to those who got them of their own volition. She did not understand how anyone could voluntarily go through the pain and other risks of getting a tattoo unless there was a good reason for it. But today's youth, and not only youth, have a simple attitude toward tattoos.

Aphrodite thought about how tattoos change in a person's skin as they age. Often, they become a disgusting sight. Only when you are young does no one want to think about it.

"Oh well. Okay, the girl suits me," thought the Goddess, turning her attention to the guy. "So, what do we have here?"

Raul was a lean, brisk, and businesslike fellow of about twenty-five. He was doing his work, measuring the statue's proportions, and did not notice the girl constantly glancing at him. Aphrodite was pleased with the observations.

"Well, I've got a classic case here: both are interested in each other but don't know how to show it. Or they can't find the right moment."

The Goddess sighed, and a light breeze blew through the hall like a draft from an open door.

"And just like that, they can walk side by side for days and months and years. And none of them will dare to say what's in their hearts. Well, my job is to help people like that, and that's what I will do."

The Goddess stopped seeing the pair of young men. Her inner gaze returned to her happy years when she loved and was loved. Only all of that was gone. The Goddess was immortal, and this immortality did not bring the oblivion that helps people move on after their losses or mistakes.

Aphrodite remembered everything that had happened in her life. And now the cheeks of the marble statue turned pink from the tenderness with which the memories of the Goddess were imbued. The statue's eyelids fluttered, and a gleam appeared in its marble eyes. A tear rolled down her cheek and landed on the girl's hand.

Paola shuddered and looked up at the statue around which she and Raul were taking measurements. The girl froze, gazing in wonder at the statue's face. The sun's rays slid across the white marble, giving it warmth and color. The figure seemed to reach out to Paola and say something.

The girl reached out to the statue and touched its marble surface. The figure was cold, and its colors were only an illusion created by the sun's slanting rays that penetrated the museum hall through an ancient window with elaborately colored stained glass. The girl shook her head, brushing those thoughts away.

"I can't be imagining all this. And I'll keep imagining things like this until I dare to tell Raul how much I like him..."

Instead of continuing her thought, the girl turned to Raul, kissing the words carelessly through tightly compressed lips.

"You know I'm tired. Let's go somewhere and have coffee."

Raul, who was at that moment behind the statue, looked out from behind it and stared at Paola with great surprise.

"To have coffee?" He said mechanically and uncertainly.

"Well, why are you repeating my words like a parrot? Yeah, we should have coffee—just the two of us. You don't have to wait for someone from your employee group to show up," Paola replied with a not-covered sarcasm.

Raul lowered both hands, holding a notebook and a pencil.

"Okay, good! Sure, we can go to the café," he said, confused.

But, of course, Aphrodite knew he liked the suggestion. The guy gathered his things into his bag, slung it over his shoulder, and looked expectantly at the girl. She also quickly gathered her belongings, which had been placed around the statue, into her large work bag and, without looking back at Aphrodite, said in a suddenly joyful voice,

"I know a cafe here that makes great coffee. You like coffee made in metal cups on hot sand, right?"

Raul suddenly lost all his exaggeratedly serious look and, with a boyish shake of his head, smiling broadly replied,

"Yes, that's the coffee I like. But how do you know that?"

The girl who had seemed so determined and collected before was embarrassed. Paola realized she had given herself away, and her sullen image disappeared. She looked into Raul's eyes and answered,

"Well... After all, I've been working beside you for a couple of months. It's been time to notice what you like."

Raul stood dumbfounded by his sudden realization. Despite her strange and gloomy image, he had always been with her, this attentive and pretty girl, and he had not even realized that she was interested in him.

"What a fool I am!" he scolded himself. "I thought she couldn't stand me."

Raul paused momentarily, then walked over to Paola and took the heavy bag of work materials from her shoulder.

The girl looked at him with a look of surprise that was immediately replaced by gratitude and understanding.

This was how it was supposed to be in her dreams. In Paola's dreams, Raul always helped her. She had surrendered to his mercy and recognized that he was a man who could help her with things she could not easily handle on her own.

But in real life, the girl showed she coped with everything alone. For example, she always carried her heavy work bags with tools by herself. Paola never gave Raul, or any of the other male colleagues on their research team, a chance to be masculine and help her. It seemed to Paola that denying her feminine nature, denying that she was physically weaker than men, was a manifestation of equality with men. However, Aphrodite knew this was not something to impress the chosen one of her hearts. If you constantly deny manhood and prevent a man from being a man, it is not equality but chaos.

There was something symbolic because Paola's bag was suddenly on the guy's shoulder. It was a victory for the Goddess of Love. That Paola had surrendered and shown her femininity for the first time since she had known Raul spoke volumes. The girl could show the man he could care for her. That was how a new love was born. Or rather, love already lived in these two's hearts. Only neither wanted to admit it.

Aphrodite thought, contemplating with a slight chuckle the newly revealed feeling these two had for each other.

"Well, another couple has been born. I don't want to think about how long their love will last. But the very birth of this feeling is a miracle of life that gives birth to a new life. Unfortunately, I am immortal, so my feelings cannot be as sharp as those of people who feel the transience of everything around them. But love is beautiful, though, for me, their love is only a moment in my life. But for these lovers, their love seems to be a lifetime long, forever. And that's what's beautiful about people. So happy that I could give them this discovery of themselves and each other!"

Aphrodite smiled contentedly. She was pleased with herself, and the day had brought her the pleasure of joining the souls of two people. She never tired of watching love find its way into people's hearts. This time, the Goddess of Love was pleased with herself and the life of these two souls who had suddenly opened themselves to each other.

While Aphrodite was immersed in her meditations on the miracle of love, the young people strolled toward the exit of the museum hall, smiling at each other and talking about something unimportant to their research work but which had become so important to them.

THE END

Written by Misha Quinn, 2023

Samantha and the Milky Way

In a valley between two ridges of mountains, in the almost total darkness of a sudden August night, a young woman sat on the edge of a large boulder. She looked up at the dark, starry sky.

Of year, in August, in the velvet darkness of night, the Milky Way spreads its wings across the entire width of the southern sky.

The starry sky beckoned and repelled Samantha. The lights of its stars glittered as if someone had lit a lamp and was trying to answer the way in the night to himself and all the travelers who had lost their way on Earth.

The young woman knew she was one of those who needed this light to find her way to happiness.

The woman recalled that long ago, when she was a child, her friend, a neighbor boy named John, had told her about the stars. He had taken astronomy lessons at school and could find all the planets and constellations visible from Earth in the night sky.

John could talk for hours about why a constellation had a name and when it was best to observe the moon or Saturn's satellites. He had no special optics for this, but he knew all about the stars and would tell Samantha all about them.

Many years had passed since the last time the friends had met. When Samantha graduated from high school and entered college, her visits to her grandmother became less and less frequent. The girl made new friends and became infatuated with one of the new acquaintances, who soon became her husband.

But life took its course, and the young family fell apart. Samantha thought she had no one who understood her like John did. But she did not know where he was. The young woman traveled alone to escape her longing and the painful memories of her failed marriage. Samantha needed to escape from everything surrounding her in her previous urban life and think about how she would live.

"Yes, where are those days of my happy childhood? And where is John, my joy and trusted friend? I don't have any of that anymore," Samantha thought as she wrapped her arms around her knees and rested her chin on her knees. "And it's all my fault."

"John must have been married a long time and have three children..." she continued wistfully musing. "And if he is, what's the use of bothering him? I left him here myself and went away to study. And I never once called him or sent him a card. I was covered in my life, and his cows and sheep no longer interested me. John never went to college to study astronomy, so he disappointed me then."

Samantha shook her head sadly as if judging herself for her choices years ago.

"I remember John saying that his family expected him to continue his father's work and become a farmer. And his younger brothers - two of them - could go to study. And that's why I need more energy to ask them where he is. I don't know what I would say to him if we met. Yeah, I'm just afraid he wouldn't even remember me. And I've been making a big deal about it, and I thought he was the only one who would understand me."

The woman lifted her head, tilted it back, and looked for familiar constellations in the insanely beautiful starry sky. But what she saw in the infinite number of stars was not constellations but John's face.

"And why don't I just go to his farm and ask his folks directly where John is and if I can see him?" Samantha thought, casting her gaze downward.

She could not see his face there anymore. She thought he was looking down at her reproachfully from that starry sky. But Samantha knew she would immediately recognize John when she saw his eyes. He had unusually kind eyes and a charming smile.

The woman tried to imagine what her friend looked like now.

“He probably has a beard and wears the same plaid shirts, jeans, and locally handmade leather boots as all his neighbors in this remote mountain area,” she thought, warmly remembering the prank rodeos John would put on for her in the sheep pen. “But it’s terrible. I haven’t seen him all grown up. I remember him as a teenager of about sixteen. Ten years have passed since then. What’s he like now? If I met him at the local supermarket, I wouldn’t recognize him even if we came face to face.”

The thought made Samantha feel cold, and she shivered, pulling her sweatshirt tighter around her. The warm summer breeze brought the spicy smells of the mountain grass still blooming on the hillsides surrounding the valley. All the scents of August nights, evenings spent with other children at her grandparents in the village, were still with Samantha.

Suddenly, she heard the rustling of leaves, which had already fallen on the grass that had long since withered on the mountainside where Samantha had settled to watch the stars and think about life. The woman turned around and saw a figure, most likely male, cautiously approaching her. Samantha instinctively gathered herself to rise and walk away.

Still, the stranger held his hand to her in a calming gesture and spoke.

“Don’t worry; I apologize for disturbing you. It’s just… I usually sit here and…”

Before he could finish speaking, Samantha jumped up from her spot on the boulder and quickly climbed down to the ground, balancing with her arms. She stood in front of the stranger and gazed into his face.

He approached her from the side and stood directly under the boulder, his face in the shadow of the enormous stone. Yes, it was impossible to see his facial features in the darkness immediately, but that voice…

Samantha was pierced, hoping she had not imagined it, and it was him, John - he was standing right in front of her and did not recognize her.

The man turned to face the starry sky and said,

"Look, over there is Cassiopeia, my favorite constellation."

The woman finally saw the features of the young man's face and, seized by a sudden rush of joy, jumped off the boulder straight to the ground, stepped toward him, and embraced him. The man stood stunned by the actions of a young woman he did not know. He moved his hands away from the woman, hesitating to touch her as she wrapped her arms around his neck and pressed her whole body against him.

"What, do I know you?" He mumbled, clearly embarrassed by the stranger's outburst.

Samantha took a step back from him and, still holding his shoulder, said,

"John, is that you?"

The man froze and, finally considering the stranger's face, stepped toward her impulsively. "Yes, that's me. Samantha?"

In his voice, there was both immense surprise and joy and hope to hear a positive answer.

The woman nodded and let go of her childhood friend's shoulder.

"So, how are you?"

There was a desire to hear that John was doing well and a lingering hope of getting information about whether he had a family.

Still smiling happily and embarrassedly, John stood before her, not knowing what to do - walk away from here and talk on the way or stay here and stare at Samantha.

Samantha repeated her question, and John, finally coming to his senses, answered.

"Yeah, I'm fine..." But some note in his voice revealed that it was not entirely true.

Samantha looked carefully into his eyes and saw an inexpressible sadness in them.

"What is it? What's the matter with you?" she said as thoughtfully as if he were still the boy with whom she shared her childhood joys and sorrows.

"It's okay. It's just that I... I haven't heard from you in so long." He replied with a smile.

Samantha raised her eyebrows in surprise, then lowered her gaze. She felt guilty that she had gone away to study and had not even said goodbye to John properly. The young woman had chosen a different path - away from the rural life of her relatives.

Since high school, Samantha had aspired to make a career. She studied for excellent grades, considering that she would have been able to enter a higher education institution only for free or with the sponsorship of a patron. The girl could indeed enroll and did not pay for her education, but she had to work nights to pay for her food and other expenses, for which her parents could not give her enough money. Her family was not wealthy - unlike the families of many of the students on the course with her.

However, her ex-husband was from a wealthy family. He decided in their relationship what, when, and how they did things with Samantha. She had little room for choice, but the young woman initially did not care because she was desperately in love with her husband. But, month after month, the relationship in their family strained. Her husband decided everything and left Samantha with little say in the matter.

Still, Samantha was entirely independent, and this disenfranchisement quickly bored her. A young woman realized it was worth thinking about divorce when her husband often left her alone at home, going to his friends' parties.

When the young couple graduated, they both got good jobs. And then Samantha realized that beyond her family, on which her husband focused her life, there was something else - freedom of choice and opinion. That was how Samantha approached the couch one evening, returning from work, on which, sprawled out and paying no attention to his wife, sat her husband.

The woman stood nearby, realized that he wasn't even thinking about taking his eyes off the TV screen, and said quietly but firmly,

"I'm leaving you."

Without waiting for an answering tirade, Samantha added,

"You'll get the details of the divorce from my lawyer. I don't want anything from you except your freedom. So you can sit here and watch TV, and I'll go to my parents' house for the night."

Her husband did not have time to reply as Samantha picked up a pre-prepared bag with her overnight guest belongings from the floor and rushed out of the living room away from the living room. She knew he would run after her. If he had not needed her as a person for quite some time, he would hire a cleaner and a cook on his considerable income. Or his family would help. That was how Samantha separated from her husband.

After that, there was a divorce, and everything went fine since they did not have children yet. However, this story, when at first you think you are loved, and then it turns out that you are just an appendix to the vast household of your spouse, left a deep trace in the soul. Samantha no longer wanted to pursue new relationships with men. Well, she was not attracted to women.

There was a faint hope in Samantha's soul that she could find her true love. And here, in an abandoned corner in the mountains, she saw again before her a man she cared for. But how did he feel? Was he asking her for this escape from the countryside to the metropolis?

John knew nothing of Samantha's thoughts. But the woman could see from his face that he was genuinely astonished and that this meeting had caused him some unexpectedly violent feelings.

"Does he really care about me?" The thought flashed somewhere in the back of Samantha's mind and suddenly glowed with rainbows and diamonds of stars comparable in beauty to the picture of the Milky Way that hung over the heads of the newly met childhood friends.

Only now Samantha saw, and not only noticed but seemed to feel with all her skin that a young and handsome man was looking at her with a look in which the joy of a new meeting replaced the past pain of parting.

Samantha gingerly touched John's hand and took his palm in her own. He seemed to allow her to do so, seemingly unwillingly. She could read nothing else on the young man's face except that he was staring at her. But the woman waited for his return move.

And it followed. John slowly leaned toward her, put his other arm around her shoulders, and touched his lips to hers. This kiss was everything Samantha had longed for - tenderness and warmth, recognition anew, and the feeling that this was how it was always supposed to be in her life.

Every kiss should have been like this - warm and waiting for her lips to respond. Samantha responded to John's kiss. Their fingers intertwined, and the tenderness of their first kiss melted their hearts and rippled through the mountain valley.

Every rock and every tree seemed at one with these people, who suddenly realized they had to be together. They did not need to say anything else. Or at least not now.

The woman and the man stood kissing under the shining stars. Their eyes were closed, but their souls were open, and their hearts beat in unison as if they were both running up the mountain - the mountain over which the Milky Way shone.

As dawn extinguished the lights of the Milky Way, the Sun took up the baton of the night, which marked a new chapter in the lives of these two who had walked so long and hard in different directions. The two humans were still there when the Sun's rays first illuminated the foothill valley containing the mountain stream swirling into a rushing river and the boulder on its bank.

Samantha and John were sitting side by side on that very boulder. His jacket carefully covered the young woman's shoulders. The man was not cold at all. He was warmed by a love whose fire had never gone out in his heart.

Yes, the man wore that plaid shirt and jeans-just as Samantha had expected. But those clothes were the very clothes Samantha wanted to see on the man next to her. And she knew she could now spend her life in complete confidence that this guy in the plaid shirt would always give her his best jacket to keep her warm.

John thought fate had brought him to this place when he had almost abandoned Samantha. And it turned out that she was waiting for him here, on this spot where he liked to spend his evenings gazing at the stars. Now, his girlfriend and future life partner sat beside him and listened to him talk about his life.

Samantha did not need to know who had been by John's side the whole time she had tried to find happiness away from him. She realized now that she was testing her fate - whether it would lead her back to John. And he, her faithful friend, was waiting for her. He was tending to his parents' farm and waiting for Samantha.

John understood perfectly well that his childhood friend needed to understand what she wanted from life - the deceptive glitz of the metropolis or the tranquility of the rural backwoods of her childhood. Only then could Samantha look at him anew and appreciate what John offered her - love, the warmth of friendship, and the security of a man's shoulder. He knew he was no match for the city dudes and rich men, but he was full of dignity. He waited for Samantha to sort out her life and return to him.

And John was right. Fate had brought them back to each other, and now Samantha did not care what she did next. She knew she needed to be there for John. She needed to be near the man who had never gotten her out of her mind and heart all this time, despite Samantha trying to change her life away from him completely.

Samantha was happy now and knew that from that moment on, her heartbeat was only for him, her faithful childhood friend and future lover, John.

THE END

Written by Misha Quinn, 2023

My dear reader, could you rate this book and leave **a good review* in this online bookstore and on Goodreads. Thank you!** If you want to read or listen to these and other short romantic stories and to know more about romance novels written by Misha Quinn, please look at Misha's website: http://www.mishaquinn.com/

You will find links to ebooks, paperbacks, large print paperback editions, and audiobooks.

The next easy-to-read short story collection with brief paragraphs, clean or sweet, with some instalove and feel-good atmosphere of each standalone, flash-fiction romantic tale is **Short Romance Stories Collection #5 (to be released in 2024)**.

My Dear Reader,

As a self-published author, I make every effort to ensure readers enjoy my books. As of this book's publication date, I do everything myself- create and write my story, covers, proofread, edit, read again, etc.

If you have any comments or suggestions about the quality of the text in this or another of my books, for example, about a phrase or word that needs to be corrected to make it sound better in context, please write your suggestions **directly to me**, via the contact form on the author's website:

http://www.mishaquinn.com/contact/

I will gladly accept your suggestions and correct the text.

Thank you in advance for your help!

Sincerely, Misha Quinn

Stay Connected with Misha Quinn

If you'd like new-release updates and occasional small gifts, you're welcome to join my newsletter:

http://www.mishaquinn.com

For readers who enjoy bonus extras and behind-the-scenes notes, I also share more on Patreon:

https://www.patreon.com/cw/mishaquinn

Welcome to the romance author's world!

Also by Misha Quinn (all series in English)

You can find all of Misha's books in many languages and other information on the author's website:

http://www.mishaquinn.com

EBOOKS & PAPERBACKS & LARGE PRINT PAPERBACKS & AUDIOBOOKS

The Salamander - A Billionaire Boss Romance Series (complete)

Sunset Lake Club - Sweet, Later-in-Life Romance and Women's Friendships Series (complete)

Sunset Lake Club LARGE PRINT Novels Editions – A Sweet, Small-Town Later-in-life Romance Series (complete)

Romance Short Story Collections: A Heartwarming, Feel-Good, Easy-Read Fiction Series – with LARGE PRINT paperback editions (each collection can be read / listening to standalone)

Throne of Flames – A Fae Fantasy Romance Series (complete)

About the Author

Misha Quinn is an independent author from Finland who has published over 25 contemporary and fantasy romance stories. She is passionate about crafting tales that entertain and inspire. Misha's heroines face challenges, grow, and ultimately find their true selves. Let these stories enrich your life, making it more exciting and fulfilling.

You can find more information about her books on her website: http://www.mishaquinn.com/

Misha also shares occasional behind-the-scenes notes and bonus content on Patreon:

https://www.patreon.com/cw/mishaquinn

www.ingramcontent.com/pod-product-compliance
Ingram Content Group UK Ltd.
Pitfield, Milton Keynes, MK11 3LW, UK
UKHW041850190726
13854UKWH00002B/807

9 798223 624189